Withdrawn

This book belongs to:

_____

SIMON SPOTLIGHT
An imprint of Simon & Schuster Children's Publishing Division
1230 Avenue of the Americas, New York, New York 10020
This Simon Spotlight edition August 2020
This book is based on the TV series PJ MASKS © Frog Box / Entertainment One UK Limited / Walt Disney EMEA Productions
Limited 2014; Les Pyjamasques by Romuald © (2007) Gallimard Jeunesse. All Rights Reserved.
This book/publication © Entertainment One UK Limited 2017.
Adapted by Maggie Testa from the series PJ MASKS.
Manufactured in China 0620 LEO
ISBN 978-1-5344-7384-3 • ISBN 978-1-5344-0615-5 (eBook)

GOOD NIGHT, HEROES

Based on the episodes "Owlette and the Owletteenies" and "Gekko and the Snore-a-saurus"

Simon Spotlight

New York London Toronto Sydney New Delhi

Today Connor, Amaya, and Greg were going on a field trip to the museum!
"I can't wait to see the Egyptian chariot," said Greg. "The teacher says it's 3,500 years old."
"And it's made of real gold," added Connor.
But when they got to the museum, their teacher had bad news. The golden chariot had vanished! It had to be the work of a nighttime villain!
"We'll find it," said Amaya. "PJ Masks, we're on our way! Into the night to save the day!"

Amaya becomes Owlette!
Greg becomes Gekko!
Connor becomes Catboy!

The PJ Masks jumped into the Owl Glider and took off, scanning the city streets. It didn't take them long to find the chariot . . . and Night Ninja. His Ninjalinos were pulling the chariot with him in it!

"Give that chariot back," said Catboy. "Or we'll have to take it."

"You don't scare me, PJ Pests. Take me for a ride, Ninjalinos, and make it fast," Night Ninja ordered.

But the Ninjalinos were tired of being bossed around. They stopped pulling the chariot.
"What's the meaning of this?" Night Ninja asked.
"Maybe they don't like how you lead them," suggested Gekko.
"I'd be a much better leader than that," said Owlette. "We'd play and have lots of fun."
The Ninjalinos ran over to Owlette. "I'll call them my Owletteenies!" she said.

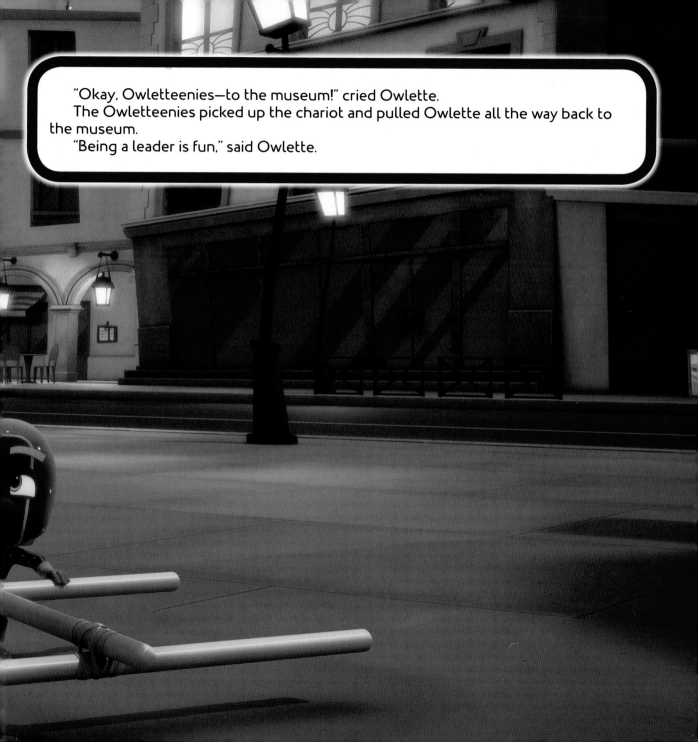

"Okay, Owletteenies—to the museum!" cried Owlette.
The Owletteenies picked up the chariot and pulled Owlette all the way back to the museum.
"Being a leader is fun," said Owlette.

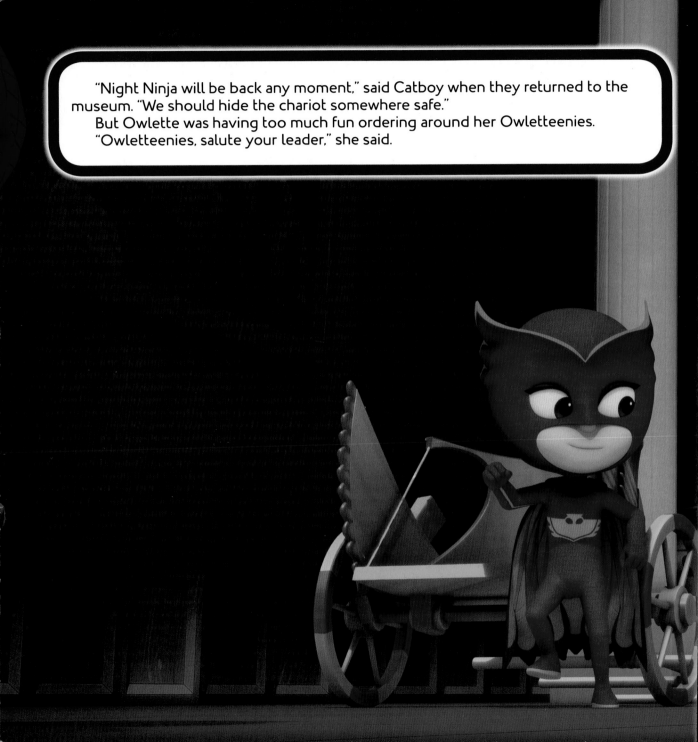

"Night Ninja will be back any moment," said Catboy when they returned to the museum. "We should hide the chariot somewhere safe."

But Owlette was having too much fun ordering around her Owletteenies. "Owletteenies, salute your leader," she said.

Owlette wasn't happy with the way they did it.

"Owletteenies, I'm your leader," she scolded them. "You need to salute me properly. One, two, three, go!"

And so the Owletteenies did just that—they went . . . away from Owlette.

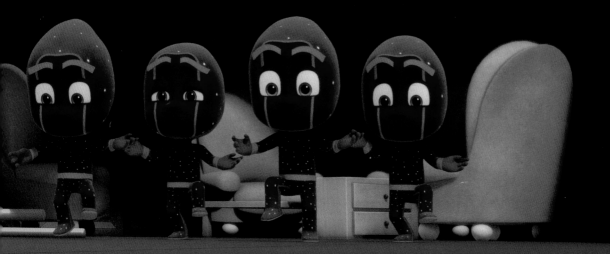

While Owlette, Catboy, and Gekko searched the museum for the Owletteenies, Night Ninja snuck in! The Owletteenies ran up to him. They decided to be Ninjalinos again. They used their Sticky-Splats to connect the chariot to a rocket ship. Now they wouldn't have to pull it!

As they blasted off, Night Ninja called out to Owlette, "So much for being a wonderful leader!"

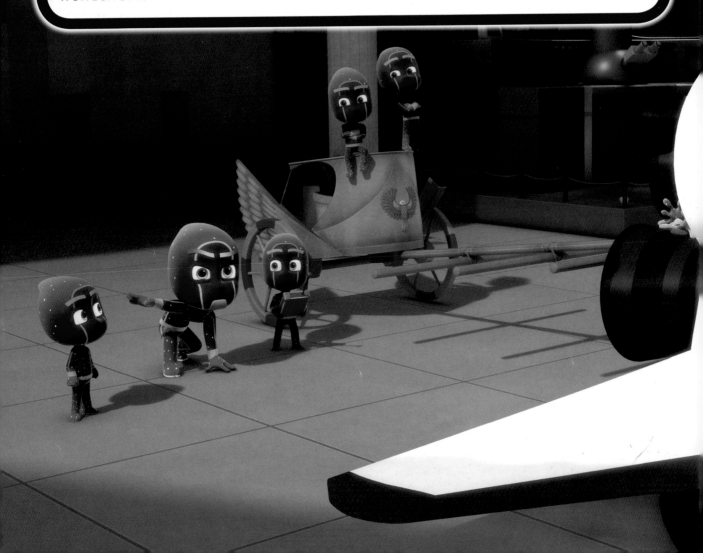

Owlette knew Night Ninja was right. "My Owletteenies are gone, and it's all my fault," she said. "Maybe they can still help us. It's time to be a hero."

The PJ Masks followed Night Ninja in the Owl Glider.

"I'm sorry, Ninjalinos," Owlette called to them. "I'm not your leader. I'm just someone who needs your help."

All of a sudden the chariot started to break away from the rocket. The Sticky-Splats were losing their stickiness!

"We're too heavy, Ninjalinos," said Night Ninja. "All of you jump out. Now!"

But the Ninjalinos were scared.

"We have to save them!" cried Owlette. She flew the Owl Glider below the chariot. The Ninjalinos landed safely.

As for Night Ninja, there was nothing he could do. The rocket sputtered down to the ground—taking him and the chariot along with it.

When the Owl Glider landed, the Ninjalinos gave Owlette a hug.

Night Ninja knew he had been wrong. "I'm sorry," he said to the Ninjalinos. He threw out his arms, and the Ninjalinos ran over to him. Night Ninja gave them a very big hug. "Oh, I love you too, my Ninjalinos," said Night Ninja.

The PJ Masks laughed. "You're really just a big softy," Owlette told him.

"Now let's get this chariot back to the museum," said Catboy.

The PJ Masks were getting tired, but their busy night wasn't over yet. Luna Girl was up to no good on the other side of town! She had taken the school's puppets, and her moths were putting on a puppet show just for her.

Gekko went to get the puppets back from Luna Girl, but he got caught up in her show.

"Woo-hoo!" he cheered at an exciting scene. That's when Luna Girl noticed him.

"Uh, give those puppets back," Gekko said, trying to sound serious.

While Gekko was running away from Luna Girl's moths, Owlette and Catboy were taking care of something else. The PJ Masks' classmate Cameron was sleepwalking around town.

"We need to get him back to bed," said Catboy.

"Yeah, but we can't use superspeed or fly him home. That would wake him up and give him a bad shock," Owlette pointed out.

Owlette and Catboy needed Gekko's help, but he had gotten away from the moths and was more interested in the puppets than in stopping Luna Girl.

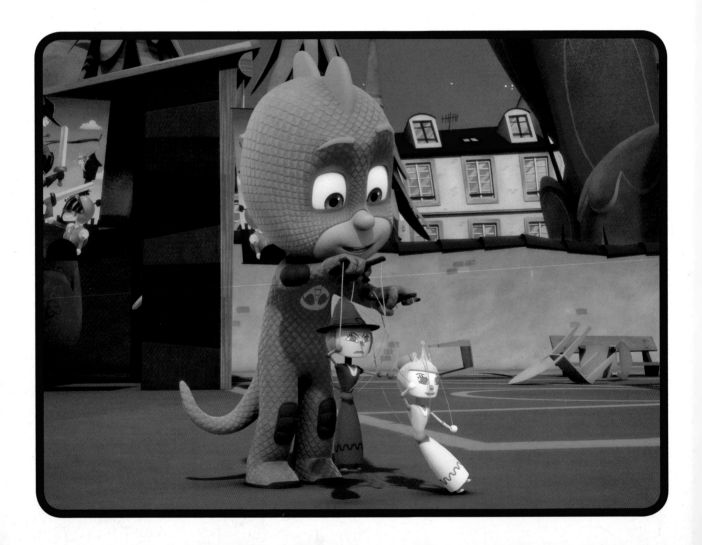

Meanwhile, Luna Girl found Cameron. Using her Luna Magnet, she turned him into a real-life puppet!

"Look at him," Luna Girl said. "He looks like a snoring dinosaur. I'm going to call him a Snore-a-saurus!"

Owlette was upset with Gekko. "Cameron wouldn't be in trouble if you hadn't been messing around with those puppets," she told him. "Are you with us?"

Gekko was determined to be a hero. Together, the PJ Masks would get Luna Girl's Luna Magnet and put Cameron back to bed without waking him up.

"Owl Wing Wind!" cried Owlette as she flapped her wings at Luna Girl. Luna Girl's moths swirled around her head. She lost control of the Luna Magnet's beam. While she was distracted, Catboy grabbed the magnet from her and threw it to Gekko.

"No, no, no, no, no!" cried Luna Girl, but there was nothing she could do. Gekko pointed the beam at Cameron and started leading him away carefully.

"Okay, let's get you to bed," said Gekko.

The night was finally quiet. Cameron was sleeping soundly in his bed, and the nighttime villains had gone home. After such a busy night, the PJ Masks sure were tired.

Owlette yawned.

Catboy yawned.

Gekko yawned.

PJ Masks all shout hooray! 'Cause in the night, we saved the day!

Good night, heroes!